ROCKET-POWERED CARS

BY

Paul Estrem

EDITED BY

Howard Schroeder, Ph.D.
Professor in Reading and Language Arts
Dept. of Curriculum and Instruction
Mankato State University

PUBLISHED BY

CRESTWOOD HOUSE

Mankato, MN, U.S.A.

CIP

LIBRARY OF CONGRESS CATALOGING IN PUBLICATION DATA

Estrem, Paul.
  Rocket-powered cars.

  (Super-charged!)
  Includes index.
  SUMMARY: Describes the characteristics of rocket-powered cars, how and why they were developed, and their uses.
  1. Automobiles, Rocket-powered—Juvenile literature. [1. Automobiles, Rocket-powered] I. Schroeder, Howard. II. Title.
TL236.E76   1987   629.2'5   87-22374
ISBN 0-89686-352-2

629.228
Estr

International Standard Book Number:	Library of Congress Catalog Card Number:
0-89686-352-2	87-22374

CREDITS

Illustrations:
Special thanks to Ky Michaelson for the photos on the following pages: Cover, 4-5, 7, 8-9, 10, 13, 14, 17, 18-19, 20-21, 22-23, 24-25, 27, 28, 30-31, 32, 33, 34, 35, 37, 38, 41, 44-45
Roy D. Query: 42
Graphic Design & Production:
Baker Street Productions, Ltd.
Technical Assistance:
Steven Jacobsen

CRESTWOOD HOUSE

Box 3427, Mankato, MN, U.S.A. 56002

TABLE OF CONTENTS

INTRODUCTION

"Mom and Dad, I see Annie!" Ellen cried as her father turned into the racetrack parking lot. "And there's Greg, working on their race car," Scott added. Annie and Greg were their next-door neighbors. Today Ellen's family was going to see them in action!

Dad parked carefully near the pit area. Mom reminded

A rocket-powered car in action is an unforgettable sight.

Ellen and Scott to be careful as they got out of the car. Race-car drivers were revving their high-powered engines in the pit area, getting ready to race. Everyone in the family put their hands over their ears. The noise was deafening!

Annie ran up to them. "Welcome to the races!" she said as she gave each of them a quick hug. "I got special passes so you can watch the action from the pit," she

added. "The four of you and Greg can watch me drive today. But before you come into the pit area, you'd better put these in your ears." Annie gave each of them a set of earplugs.

"This is much better," Mom said loudly after she put in her earplugs. "But those engines are still very noisy!"

Annie laughed and said, "You haven't heard anything yet. A rocket-powered dragster is here for an exhibition run today. These engines are quiet compared to a rocket!"

"I thought rockets were used only in the air. How do they stay on the ground?" Scott asked with a puzzled look on his face. "That's a good question," Annie replied, "and you'll get the answer soon. But right now, let's go see if Greg has tuned up our 'rail' for my race!"

Greg waved and smiled when he saw Annie and their neighbors walking toward him through the pit area. He greeted everyone and then said, "Annie, it's time to strap in and get ready to roll. You're up in five minutes." Greg helped Annie put on her fireproof racing suit, boots, gloves, and helmet. Then he helped her get into the cockpit of their sleek red-and-black dragster. He secured the safety harness as two crew members checked the machine over one last time.

Greg and the pit crew pushed the dragster to the starting line from the pit. Annie turned and waved at the family as the big engine roared to life. "I can't believe that's Annie driving that thing," Dad exclaimed. "It

A rocket-powered dragster is long and narrow, with wide rear tires.

Regular dragsters are always fun to watch—but a rocket-powered dragster is a real crowd pleaser!

is, Dad,'' Ellen replied, ''and we'd better hope that she knows how to drive it well.''

Greg overheard Ellen's remark and laughed as he walked back to the pit. ''Don't worry, Ellen,'' he said. ''Annie is one of the best drivers in the business. She's had a lot of practice, is very careful, and knows exactly what she's doing. Watch the race, and you'll see what I mean.''

Just then, Annie and the driver next to her revved

their engines to a loud roar. The starting light turned green and two smoke clouds were thrown out behind the racers from their tires and exhaust. They were off! And in just a few seconds, their parachutes were out and the race was over. Annie's red-and-black dragster had crossed the finish line a split second sooner than the other dragster. She'd won! Greg and the rest of the crew ran out to meet Annie on her trip back from the finish line.

With Annie at the wheel and the engine turned off, Greg and his crew pushed the dragster back into the pit. "That was terrific!" Ellen exclaimed as she ran up to the sleek racing machine. Annie took off her helmet and laughed. "Not quite what I wanted, Ellen, but pretty close." She unhooked her safety harness and climbed out of the cockpit. "It looked like you were going to take off into the air," Scott said.

"Your ET (elapsed time) was one full second better than last weekend, Annie," Greg said. "And your control was much better off the line. Remember how it

Take off!

almost got away from you last time? Next weekend will be even better.''

Just then they heard a deep sound, like thunder. Turning their heads, they saw a bright flash of fire at the far end of the pit. The noise stopped just as quickly as it had begun.

''The rocket car!'' Annie exclaimed. ''Come on, everybody, Greg and I don't want you to miss this. Dragsters like ours are neat, but rocket power is out of this world!''

Mom, Dad, Ellen, and Scott quickly followed Annie and Greg through the crowd to the edge of the pit. They stopped at a rope fence about fifty yards (46 m) from a shiny yellow dragster on the racetrack. Strange-looking tanks were mounted on the car. The rear end looked like the bottom of a spaceship. Several crew members were pushing the car into the starting position. Then they ran to the sidelines.

''Why are all the crew members getting away from the back of the car?'' Ellen asked. ''You'll see why in a few seconds,'' Annie replied. The crowd became quiet.

Suddenly, a thirty-foot (9.1 m) flame shot out of the back of the rocket car. It sounded like thunder! And then the loud sound of the rocket engine turned into a high-pitched howl. The dragster shot down the track like an arrow, with all four wheels on the ground. Within seconds, its parachute was out and the exhibition run was over. It had been easy to see how much faster the rocket car was than the other dragsters.

"How did you like that, kids?" Annie said, laughing. "When it comes to speed, nothing compares to a rocket—in the air, in space, or even on the ground!"

WHAT IS A ROCKET-POWERED CAR?

Unless you already know about rocket-powered cars, you probably have many of the same questions that Ellen and Scott had after seeing one in action. We'll be looking at specific types of car races, racing cars and racing engines on the following pages. But first, let's start with the basics.

Cars with standard engines and transmissions are called "wheel-driven" cars. The engine provides power, which is carried to the transmission. Then the transmission turns one or more wheels, which make the car move. Most wheel-driven cars can also move in reverse.

Rocket-powered cars are not wheel-driven. They move forward only when the rocket forces air backward. When fuel is fed to the rocket, the car blasts ahead at high speed. The only way to slow down is to turn down or shut off the fuel supply. There is no gear shifting or reverse gear in rocket-powered cars, since a rocket only pushes air in one direction. You either feed fuel to the rocket or shut it down and put on the brakes!

Ky Michaelson's Conklin Comet sits apart from its body, showing a carefully designed frame.

13

Another difference is that wheel-driven cars are easier to steer. Because power is provided through the wheels, the speed and direction of the cars can be controlled by shifting. A rocket-powered car has only two speeds: fast and faster! And since the rocket does not provide power to the wheels, the wheels must follow the same course as the rocket. The natural motion of any rocket is straight ahead, so rocket-powered cars are run only in ''straight-line'' racing events. The two main events in which rocket-powered cars compete are drag racing and the world land-speed-record competition. The rocket-powered cars most often win!

The fuel tank is one of the most important parts of any rocket-powered car.

ROCKETS AND JETS

Rocket-powered cars are certainly fast—but they do have some competition. Between 1963 and 1970, the world's land-speed record was most often held by jet-powered cars. In fact, today's official world record is held by the "Thrust 2," a jet-powered car from England.

Like rocket-powered cars, jet-powered cars are not wheel driven. There are differences, though. Rockets are different from jets in the following ways:

First, jet engines are designed for ongoing use, like a jet airplane. They provide a lot of energy by burning a very high-powered fuel at a steady rate. Their speed is controlled by increasing or decreasing the amount of fuel burned. One danger is that the fuel can explode very easily.

Rockets, on the other hand, are designed to produce a short blast with a lot of power. To understand the difference in power, remember that a jet engine is not able to push a space vehicle out of the earth's atmosphere. A rocket engine, however, can provide the needed power.

How do rockets provide more power than jet engines? It comes down to the way the fuel is used. Jets use combustion (burning) of fuel, while rockets use a different process. In rockets, hydrogen peroxide (H_2O_2), a watery liquid, is broken down into its two parts: water and oxygen. A great amount of heat is created by this process. The heat then produces steam, which passes through the rocket nozzle at a very high speed. This produces the forward movement of the rocket.

Solid fuel was used in the first rocket-powered cars. But the drivers soon found that the fuel was used up too fast. They would often run out of fuel before the end of the race. The solid fuel also made the rocket more difficult to control. After some experimenting, the drivers found out that liquid fuel could be used to provide the greatest amount of control. Before long, rocket-powered cars were often beating cars with both jet and conventional engines. The rocket age of racing had begun!

ROCKET-POWERED HISTORY

The first known rocket-powered race car was invented by Fritz von Opel, a German, in the 1920's. His car looked like a long bullet, with short wings behind the front wheels. Explosive powder was used as rocket fuel. Von Opel's rocket-powered car was clocked at over 125 miles (200 km) per hour. The car was not a great success, since the land-speed record for wheel-driven race cars at that time was over 200 miles (322 km) per hour.

No one tried to beat von Opel's rocket-powered land-speed-record attempt for almost forty years. Then, in 1965, Walt Arfons tried to capture the record with his

A rocket is made to produce a short blast with a lot of power.

On long, flat tracks, land-speed-record drivers try to "beat the clock."

solid-fuel, rocket-powered "Wingfoot Express II" on the Bonneville salt flats. The car went as fast as 580 miles (933 km) per hour, but the solid fuel burned out too fast. And besides, the jet-powered racers were going faster than 600 miles (965 km) per hour at the time. The power of rockets was known, but the engineers didn't quite know how to make use of all that power yet.

THE LAND-SPEED-RECORD RACE

Stock-car racing, motocross racing, and bicycle racing all have one thing in common: Drivers are competing side by side against each other. The world's land-speed-record (LSR) race is different: Each driver competes directly with the clock. All you need to beat the land-speed record is a clock, a long, flat track, nerves of steel—and the world's fastest race car!

The Bonneville Speedway on the salt flats of Utah is the most popular land-speed-record track. At one time, Bonneville Lake covered hundreds of square miles in the Southwest. The lake eventually dried up, leaving a flat, dry surface of salt. This salt surface is ideal for driving land-speed-record cars at very high speeds. Several other tracks have also been used by land-speed-record challengers. These tracks are in California, Florida, Nevada, England, Wales and Australia.

The ten-mile (16 km) track at Bonneville is flat and

In 1970, Gary Gabelich and the Blue Flame took the racing world by surprise with a new land-speed record of over 622 miles (1,000 km) per hour.

straight. A dark, straight line is painted down the center of the track so the driver won't go to the left or right at high speeds. Despite the most careful safety precautions, the Bonneville track has been the site of many tragic crashes. At speeds faster than 600 miles (965 km) per hour, one small mistake can turn into a disaster.

So how are land-speed records made and broken? The Federation Internationale de l'Automobile (F.I.A.) is recognized throughout the world as the major organization that determines the winner. To win the land-speed record, a driver must make two runs on an approved

The Blue Flame was a little over 38 feet (11.6 m) long—with a rocket engine that could produce up to 35,000 horsepower.!

track: one trip down and one trip back. The average of the two top speeds clocked is the official top speed.

Can you visit Bonneville to watch a land-speed-record challenger? You would be lucky, indeed, to see one of these important runs at Bonneville. Most often, the top land-speed-record teams go to the flats when there are no big races scheduled. That way, they can be sure that a stray spectator won't wander onto the track during a run!

TWO ROCKET-POWERED STARS

Now let's take a close look at the two major rocket-powered land-speed-record cars that have made racing history: the Blue Flame and the Budweiser Rocket.

The Blue Flame

After the unsuccessful attempts of Fritz von Opel (1920's) and Walt Arfons (1965), a rocket-powered

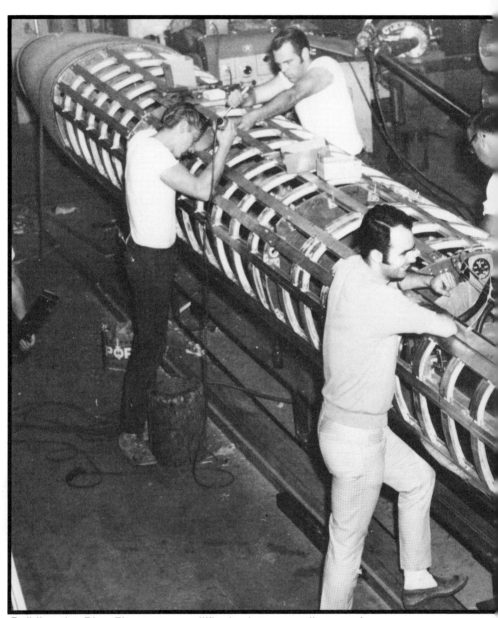

Building the Blue Flame was a difficult—but rewarding—task.

land-speed-record car did not run again until 1970. In that year, the Blue Flame appeared at Bonneville. Built by Reaction Dynamics, Inc. of Milwaukee, Wisconsin, the Blue Flame was piloted by Gary Gabelich, an experienced and daring race driver.

The Blue Flame was a little more than thirty-eight feet (11.6 m) long and weighed almost three tons (2.7 MT). It was powered by a liquid-fuel rocket engine that was thought to produce at least 35,000 horsepower! The tires were handmade with extra-thin treads. They were inflated to 350 pounds per square inch (psi). (Regular car tires are inflated to no more than 35 psi.) The car was shaped like a missile, with a large tail section sticking up.

After a few weeks of test runs and final adjustments, Gabelich piloted the Blue Flame to an astounding new record: 622.407 miles (1,001 km) per hour. He had beaten Craig Breedlove's jet-powered LSR car by a full 22 miles (35 km) per hour. A rocket had taken the lead!

The Budweiser Rocket

Nine full years after the Blue Flame's land-speed-record triumph, the Budweiser Rocket appeared at Bonneville. It was smaller than the Blue Flame, although it, too, was shaped like a missile. This rocket-powered car caused a stir that is still discussed in official racing circles.

A three-wheeler, the Budweiser Rocket was a little over thirty-nine feet (11.9 m) long. The rear wheels were solid discs weighing one hundred pounds (45 kg)

Stan Barrett and the Budweiser Rocket broke the sound barrier in 1979. The racing world has never been the same!

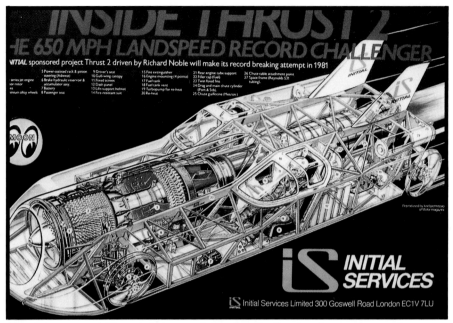

The jet-powered *Thrust 2* is a mighty foe in the land-speed-record challenge.

each. The rocket itself was estimated to produce at least 48,000 horsepower. Also, a ''sidewinder'' missile was actually fired from the car during its runs to provide an extra six thousand pounds of thrust! The machine was piloted by Stan Barrett, an expert stuntman and race driver.

No one argues with the fact that the Budweiser Rocket is the fastest rocket-powered car in the world. The problem is that some groups don't agree with the judging methods used at the Budweiser Rocket speed trials. Some sources recognize the Rocket as having taken the

28

land-speed record in 1979 with a speed of 638.64 miles (1,028 km) per hour. Others ignore that run. They say that a jet-powered car, the Thrust 2, captured the land-speed record in 1983 with a speed of 633.47 miles (1,019 km) per hour.

Most experts agree, however, that the Budweiser Rocket ran an accurately clocked speed of 739.67 miles (1,190 km) per hour at Edwards Air Force Base, California, in 1979. Many people think that this speed broke the sound barrier. It was also the fastest speed ever recorded for a wheeled land vehicle! It is not the official record, though, since the speed was not recorded as an official two-run average.

ROCKET-POWERED DRAGSTERS

Like land-speed-record racing, most drag racing is run directly against the clock. A drag race is a short, straight-line race, most often the distance of a quarter mile (402 m). The only rules are to go on the green light and follow the straight line in the middle of the track. But don't forget to stop! Most dragsters have parachutes or other braking devices to help them slow down at the end of the quarter mile.

The rear tires of a dragster are large and wide. They have little or no tread to provide the best traction on pavement. The front tires are very lightweight, almost like bicycle tires. The engine and driver are most often sitting toward the rear of the machine, so heavy front wheels are not needed for support.

Dragsters, or "rails," have powerful engines. They are tuned to provide high acceleration over a short stretch. In fact, most drag races last less than ten seconds!

Like rocket-powered land-speed-record cars, rocket-powered dragsters simply can't be matched. Since rocket engines provide full power very quickly, they

After a successful run, the Conklin Comet uses its parachute to slow down.

leave wheel-driven dragsters in the dust! For example, Don Garlits holds the world record of 268 miles (431 km) per hour in the quarter-mile (402 m) run with a wheel-driven machine. Kitty O'Neil holds the rocket-powered record of 392.54 miles (632 km) per hour! Also, the lowest elapsed time (ET) for a wheel-driven dragster is 5.39 seconds. This record was set by Gary Beck in 1983. Kitty O'Neil's record for a rocket-powered dragster is 3.72 seconds!

ROCKET-POWERED FUNNY CARS

Before rocket-powered cars were invented, ''Funny Cars'' were a big attraction at drag races. What's the difference between a dragster and a Funny Car? Not much. All the makings of a dragster are hidden beneath the lightweight body of a stock American-made car. The driver usually sits toward the rear of the body, where the back seat should be. A Funny-Car race is the same as a drag race: The highest speed and lowest ET in the quarter mile (402 m) wins. Rocket-powered Funny Cars are now the main novelty attraction at drag races. The other cars simply don't have a chance to keep up with them!

Jim Hodges stands proudly by his rocket-powered Funny Car, the Alabama Express.

OTHER ROCKET-POWERED VEHICLES

As you can see, rocket power has taken the straight-line racing world by storm. If a jet-powered machine wins an event or record, there's sure to be a rocket-powered contender close behind! This is true for other vehicles, too. Let's take a look at some of them:

Rocket-Powered Snowmobile

The "X-1," a rocket-powered dragster built by Reaction Dynamics, Inc., was converted into the Sonic Challenger, a rocket-powered snowmobile. This machine was officially clocked at 114 miles (183 km) per hour!

The Sonic Challenger is probably the fastest snowmobile around!

Ky Michaelson's rocket-powered motorcycle is nearly always a winner.

Rocket-Powered Motorcycle
Ky Michaelson of Space Age Racing, Inc., built a rocket-powered motorcycle that has seldom been beaten.

Rocket-Powered Go-Kart
This rocket-powered go-kart, driven by Pat Best, was clocked at a record 246 miles (396 km) per hour.

Rocket-Powered Roller Skates!
Wearing a rocket-powered "backpack" and roller skates, Curt Michaelson can zoom along at speeds up to 52 miles (84 km) per hour.

Wearing a rocket-powered backpack and roller skates, Curt Michael-son shows that he isn't afraid of a little speed!

ROCKET SAFETY

From roller skates to the big land-speed-record challengers, the risks of working with rocket power are obvious. It's important to remember that all the people involved in these high-powered projects are trained professionals. As such, they have their own set of rigid safety standards.

Even with many safety measures, some drivers and

assistants have been seriously injured. A few have lost their lives. The early days of drag racing were especially marked by accidents that could have been prevented. Today, the organizations that sponsor high-powered racing activities have strict safety standards for car builders, drivers, and pit crews. Overall, professional racing is now among the most safety-conscious sports in the world.

Organizations such as the American Hot Rod Association (AHRA), National Hot Rod Association (NHRA), and International Hot Rod Association (IHRA) were originally formed to help develop and enforce safety standards. Especially with rocket power, car builders and drivers have now learned the most valuable safety measures of other high-powered fields. Other fields closely related to rocket technology include the aircraft, aerospace, and computer technology industries.

Rocket-powered-car owners, drivers, and pit crews must be just as well trained and disciplined as airline pilots in order to avoid needless accidents. When accidents occur, they can be serious for everyone. The safety guidelines below show how serious today's car builders, drivers, and pit crews are about their safety—and the safety of others.

The Drivers

Most often, rocket-powered-car pilots are seasoned race-car drivers. They already understand the importance of racing safety. Car owners always select their drivers carefully, since the owners have made a costly investment in their machines. For talented but inexperienced drivers, race-car driving schools can provide the training needed to get started. This is a good idea for any serious driver, because official races require proof of driver fitness before racing.

The Drivers' Clothing

In sanctioned racing, drivers are required to wear fireproof clothing. You will most often see drivers wearing one-piece fireproof suits. These suits protect the driver from fire and heat, and also provide freedom of movement. Approved helmets, faceguards or goggles, gloves, and boots are also required.

A good race-car driver needs talent and experience—and these world-record holders are among the best. From left to right: Ky Michaelson, Dave Anderson, Paula Murphy, Gary Gabelich, and Art Arfons. 37

Rocket power can be very dangerous, and everyone involved needs to be prepared for emergencies. Note the ambulance standing ready behind the Conklin Comet.

The Race Cars

Like other race cars, rocket-powered cars must be built to meet safety requirements. Physical protection around the driver should include a strong roll-bar system. If the car overturns or rolls, the roll bars will help protect the driver. Also, race cars must have fire-fighting equipment within the driver's reach. Funny Cars, especially, are required to have two exits so the driver can escape during an accident or fire. Other safety requirements include special floorboards, window materials, and instrument placement.

One of the most important safety features of a rocket-powered race car is the parachute braking system. Rocket cars accelerate very fast. They must also be able to stop before they reach the end of the track. Most rocket-powered cars have parachute systems with built-in safeguards.

The Pit Crew

Each crew member must be prepared for any emergency that might occur during or after a race. You will usually see a lot of fire-control equipment around the pit area at a racetrack. Crew members are often required to know emergency first aid.

The pit crew is also responsible for the condition of the race car itself. Crew members are hired for their experience, know-how and ability to think fast in tough situations. The sharp eye of a crew member has saved a driver's life more than once, simply by spotting a loose bolt, connector, or fuel line.

The Track Staff

Racetracks are required to have emergency and fire-control equipment and workers on hand. Even if there are no accidents, you will see fire trucks and ambulances standing ready during racing events. The track staff is also responsible for making sure that all track equipment is working properly and that the track is in excellent condition.

THE ROCKET-POWERED FUTURE!

J.R. Cobb's "Railton" set the wheel-driven land-speed record of 394.20 miles (634 km) per hour in 1947. At that time, Cobb probably never thought that his record would be beaten by a jet-powered car. Then along came Craig Breedlove's "Spirit of America" in 1963. In the same way, Breedlove probably never thought that his 1965 jet-powered record of 600.60 miles (966 km) per hour would be beaten by a rocket! But along came Gary Gabelich and the Blue Flame in 1970.

Then, of course, Stan Barrett and the Budweiser Rocket came on the scene in 1979. No matter how unofficial the results were, the 739.67 miles (1,190 km) per hour clocked at Edwards Air Force Base astounded the racing world. What's next? The exciting thing about racing is that anything is possible. Perhaps Craig Breedlove is working on a new car in an old abandoned hangar somewhere in Nevada. Maybe Stan Barrett has decided to return to racing. Ky Michaelson could have the answer in the new rocket-powered car he's building. Or perhaps Kitty O'Neil is getting ready to shock the world again.

A few things are certain: As long as there is some uncertainty about the Budweiser Rocket breaking the sound barrier, someone else will try for the official record. And as long as there are rockets, there will be

Kitty O'Neil knows that when it comes to rocket-powered racing, anything is possible!

The battle between rockets and jets will probably create excitement for years to come. Shown above is Craig Breedlove's jet-powered car, the Spirit of America.

rocket-powered cars. The next earth-shaking rocket-powered feat is probably just around the corner.

WHERE TO LEARN MORE

Like Ellen and Scott, maybe you've had your first taste of rocket-powered excitement. Or maybe you've never seen a race but are interested in this fast-paced sport. How can you learn more?

One way is to visit a drag strip or other racing facility in your area. You will be able to meet many people who love "straight-line" racing—and especially rocket-powered racing! They will be happy to tell you about upcoming events.

Contacting a local chapter of the American Hot Rod Association (AHRA), the National Hot Rod Association (NHRA), or other car-racing interest groups can also help you learn about racing. You can find a lot of information in the hot-rod and race-car magazines found on any well-stocked magazine rack, as well. This way, you can contact national organizations and keep up with the latest developments in the world of rocket-powered racing.

One thing is certain: The thrills and excitement of rocket-powered cars are here to stay!

A rocket-powered car prepares to thrill its many fans.

GLOSSARY / INDEX

AHRA 36, 43 — *Abbreviation for "American Hot Rod Association."*

COCKPIT 6, 10 — *Driver's compartment in a race car.*

DRAG RACE 14, 29, 30, 32, 36 — *A high-speed race on a straight track.*

DRAG STRIP 43 — *A flat, straight racetrack designed specifically for straight-line racing. The track is usually one-quarter mile (402 m) long.*

DRAGSTER 6, 9, 10, 11, 12, 29, 30, 31, 32, 33 — *An extremely powerful race car built only for straight-line drag racing.*

ET 10, 31, 32 — *Abbreviation for "elapsed time." The time from the start to the end of a race.*

F.I.A. 21 — *The Federation Internationale de l'Automobile (International Automobile Federation). An organization that judges and determines international motor-sport records.*

FUNNY CAR 32, 38 — *A dragster with a full-size car body.*

GO-KART 34 — *A small, motorized four-wheel racing car.*

GLOSSARY / INDEX

HYDROGEN PEROXIDE 15 — *A watery substance used as rocket fuel.*

IHRA 36 — *Abbreviation for "International Hot Rod Association."*

LSR 19, 26 — *Abbreviation for "Land-Speed Record."*

NHRA 36, 43 — *Abbreviation for "National Hot Rod Association."*

OFF THE LINE 10 — *The beginning of a straight-line race, when the judges begin to clock the elapsed time.*

PIT 5, 6, 8, 10, 11, 39 — *Area where mechanics work on race cars at a racetrack before and between races.*

RAIL 6, 30 — *Nickname for "dragster."*

REV 5, 8 — *To accelerate, or speed up, a motor or engine.*

STRAIGHT-LINE RACING 14, 43 — *Racing in which drivers try to achieve the fastest speed in the shortest amount of time. The track is flat and straight.*

TRACTION 29 — *Gripping power, as in tire treads gripping the pavement.*